This book belongs to:

....

....

Editor: Alexandra Koken
Designer: Plum Pudding Design

Copyright © QED Publishing 2012

This edition published 2012 for Index Books

First published in the UK in 2012 by QED Publishing
A Quarto Group company, 230 City Road, London EC1V 2TT

www.qed-publishing.co.uk

A catalogue record for this book is available from the British Library.

ISBN 978 1 84835 986 4

Printed in China

Listen Up, Pup!

Steve Smallman and Gill McLean

QED Publishing

Toby was a happy dog.
His people were well trained.
They took him for walks...

...tickled his tummy...

...let him lie on the sofa and, every now and then, gave him a sausage. Yes, life was good.

Until Snoop came along!
Snoop was a cute and fluffy puppy.
Toby didn't like him.

Snoop ran up to Toby, wagging his tail.
Toby barked at Snoop...

...and his people sent Toby to his basket.

"What do they want another dog for?"
Toby grumbled to himself.
"What's the matter with me?"

Toby had a long think. Then he sneaked out of his
basket and over to the puppy.
But this time he didn't bark at Snoop...

...he licked him right on the nose!

"Good boy!" cried his people and gave him a sausage.
"Mmmmm", thought Toby. "Interesting."

"Listen up, Pup," said Toby the next day.
"If you're staying, there are a few things you need to learn."

"Lesson one: this is MY basket, keep out of it!"

"Lesson two: this is MY food bowl, keep out of that, too!"

"Lesson three: always make a fuss
of your people when they come home.

You could get a sausage.
But try not to pee on the floor!"

"Lesson four: always let them
know when it's time for walkies...

...they sometimes forget."

"Lesson five: as soon as they take off your lead, run to the pond."

"Can I jump in?"
asked Snoop.

"No, but it's fun to
scatter the ducks!"
said Toby.

"Lesson six: you can roll around in
poop if you want to – it makes you smell nice!"

"But not everyone thinks so."

"Well done, Pup," said Toby. "That's all for now."
"What about chasing?" asked Snoop.

"Chasing?" said Toby. "Well, all right.
You can go first if you like."

And the two dogs chased
each other...

...until they were tired and happy and dizzy.

Toby flopped wearily into his basket.
Snoop forgot all about lesson one and climbed in too!

But before Toby even had a
chance to complain, his people
scratched his ears and smiled.

"All right, Pup," Toby whispered. "You can stay."
And they both fell fast asleep.

Next steps

Show the children the cover again. Could the children have guessed what the story is about? Read the title together; does that give them a clue?

When the children have read the story, or you have read it to them, ask them why Toby didn't like the puppy at first.

Do the children think Toby liked Snoop at the end of the story?

If so, what made Toby change his mind?

Ask the children if any of them have little brothers or sisters.

Do the children sometimes get a bit jealous if Mum or Dad pay lots of attention to a brother or sister?

Do you think that Toby and Snoop will stay friends even if the sausages run out?

Ask the children to draw a picture of Toby and Snoop.